The Monster Bed

The artist gratefully acknowledges the permission granted by Maurice Sendak for the use of characters from Where the Wild Things Are, © 1963 by Maurice Sendak.

Published by Hinkler Books Pty Ltd
45–55 Fairchild Street
Heatherton Victoria 3202 Australia
www.hinklerbooks.com

First published by Andersen Press Ltd., London

Text © Jeanne Willis 1986
Illustrations © Susan Varley 1986
Cover design © Hinkler Books 2010

Cover design: Peter Tovey
Prepress: Graphic Print Group

ISBN: 978 1 7418 4435 1

Printed and bound in China

The Monster Bed

Jeanne Willis and Susan Varley

HB
HINKLER
BOOKS

Never go down to the Withering Wood,

The goblins and ghoulies are up to no good.

The gnomes are all nasty, the trolls are all hairy

And even the pixies and fairies are scary.

Oh, never go down there, unless you are brave,

In case you discover the Cobbeldy Cave.

For inside that cave which is gloomy and glum

Live Dennis the monster and Dennis's mum.

Now Dennis the monster was mostly polite;

He tried very hard not to bellow and bite,

Except, I'm afraid, when the time came for bed.

"I'm frightened! I'm frightened!" the wee monster said.

"But why?" asked his mummy. "There's nothing to fear,
I've given you teddy, the light switch is here."

"The humans will get me," cried Dennis. "They'll creep
Under my monster bed, when I'm asleep."

"Oh, no," said his mummy, "I cannot agree,
There are no human beings, what fiddle-dee-fee.
They are only in stories. They do not exist.
Now get into bed and be quiet and kissed."

But when she bent down to kiss Dennis, he chose

To fasten his fangs round her warty old nose.

He tied up his toes in a knot round her knees.

"Led go of be, Deddid, you're hurtig be, please!"

"Only," he said, "if you help with my plan."

"All right," squealed his mummy, "I will if I can."

"Please take off my pillows and blankets," he said.

"From now on, I'd rather sleep under my bed,

For if I am there and a human comes near

It won't think to look for me, safe under here."

So there Dennis lay, staring up at the springs,
Thinking of birthdays, and chocolate and things.

Now a certain small boy who played truant from school
Got lost in the wood, in the dark—little fool!

And feeling so tired he could wander no more

He stopped at the cave and he went through the door.

He saw the bare mattress, and desperate for rest

He peeled off his wellies and stripped to his vest.

He laid himself down and he shivered with fright.

He wished that his mummy could kiss him goodnight

And check that no monsters were under the bed.

But she wasn't there . . .

SO HE DID IT INSTEAD!

The End